To my children, who were the inspiration
for this story, and their dad

B. S. H.

To Mother Earth,
who gives so much
and is given so little

E. Y.

BY *Barbara Savadge Horton*

ILLUSTRATED BY *Ed Young*

ALFRED A. KNOPF NEW YORK

THIS IS A BORZOI BOOK PUBLISHED BY ALFRED A. KNOPF, INC.

Published in the United States by Alfred A. Knopf, Inc., New York, and simultaneously in Canada by Random House of Canada Limited, Toronto. Distributed by Random House, Inc., New York.

Manufactured in the United States of America
10 9 8 7 6 5 4 3 2 1

Library of Congress Cataloging-in-Publication Data
Horton, Barbara Savadge

What comes in spring? / by Barbara Savadge Horton ; illustrated by Ed Young. p. cm.
Summary: A mother explains to her daughter how she grew inside her as the seasons changed, bringing great happiness to Mama and Daddy both at her birth and now.
ISBN 0-679-80268-1 (trade) ISBN 0-679-90268-6 (lib. bdg.)
[1. Seasons—Fiction. 2. Reproduction—Fiction. 3. Mothers and daughters—Fiction.]
I. Young, Ed, ill. II. Title. PZ7.H7919Wh 1992 [E]—dc20 89-39695

"Mama, what comes in spring?"

"Flowers come
and leaves on trees
and robins come in spring."

"The first time I ever saw your daddy
it was spring."

"Where was I?"

"You weren't born yet."

"Mama, what comes next?"

"Summer comes next.
A warm wind blows,
and the sun is hot.
In summer the ice-cream man
rings his bell,
and you have to eat a Popsicle
to cool off."

"In summer we build a fire outdoors
and roast hot dogs for dinner
and toast marshmallows
till they're sticky sweet
for dessert.
Then we lie on our backs in the grass
to watch the stars come out."

"In summer I married your daddy."

"Where was I?"

"You weren't born yet."

"Mama, what comes next?"

"Autumn comes next.
The leaves turn orange,
yellow, red.
One by one they kite down
from the trees, and we
rake them up
and jump into the piles
and listen to the noise they make,
like paper crumpling,
like fire crackling,
underneath our feet.
The wind turns cool.
Big kids go to school."

"In autumn you started to grow
inside of me."

"In autumn I started to grow.
Mama, what comes next?"

“Winter comes next.
The wind turns cold.
It snows.
You get to wear a snowsuit
and new mittens
and boots,

and every step you take
makes tracks,
and every breath you take
makes smoke."

"It seems the whole world's white
and when the sun shines
in the crisp, clean air,
the snow sparkles
and when you shout my name
and I shout yours,
our voices sound loud
in the quiet."

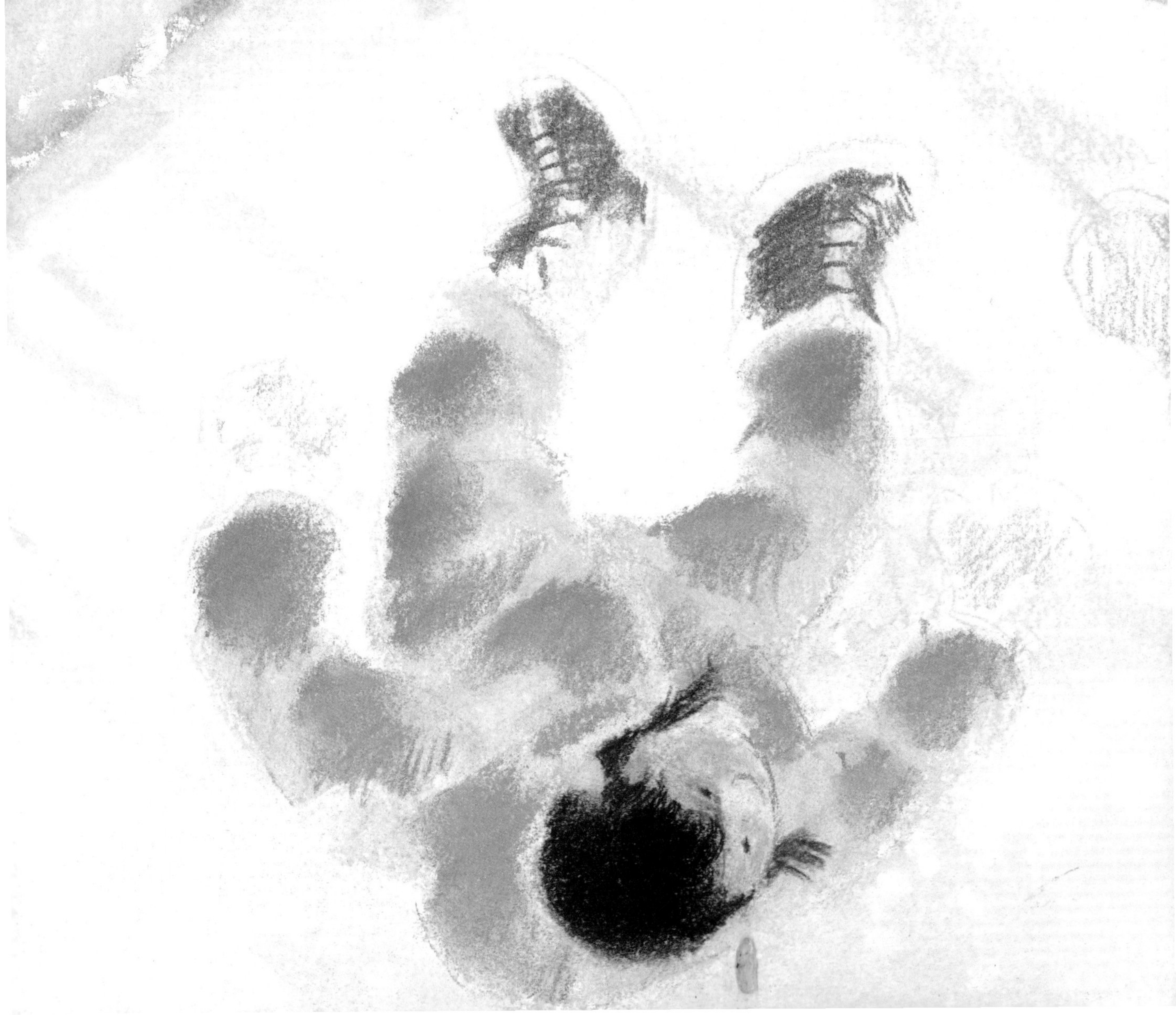

"In winter you grew big inside of me."

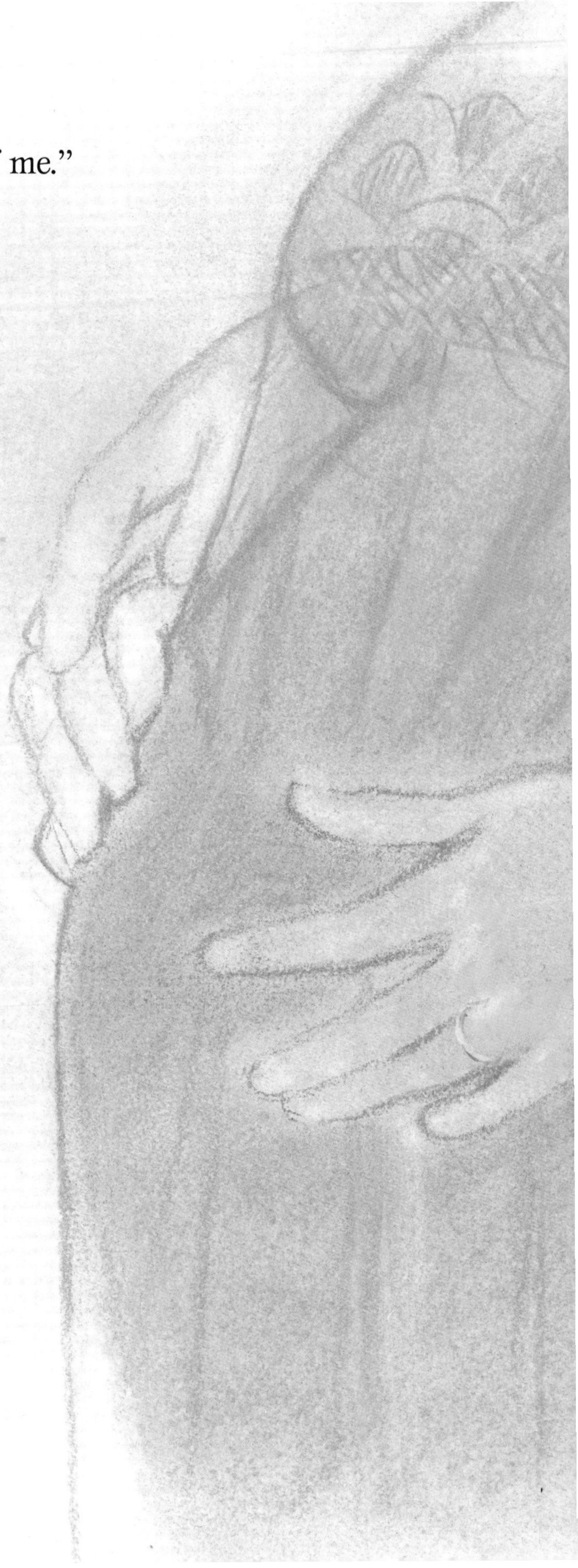

"In winter I grew big
inside of you.
Mama, what comes next?"

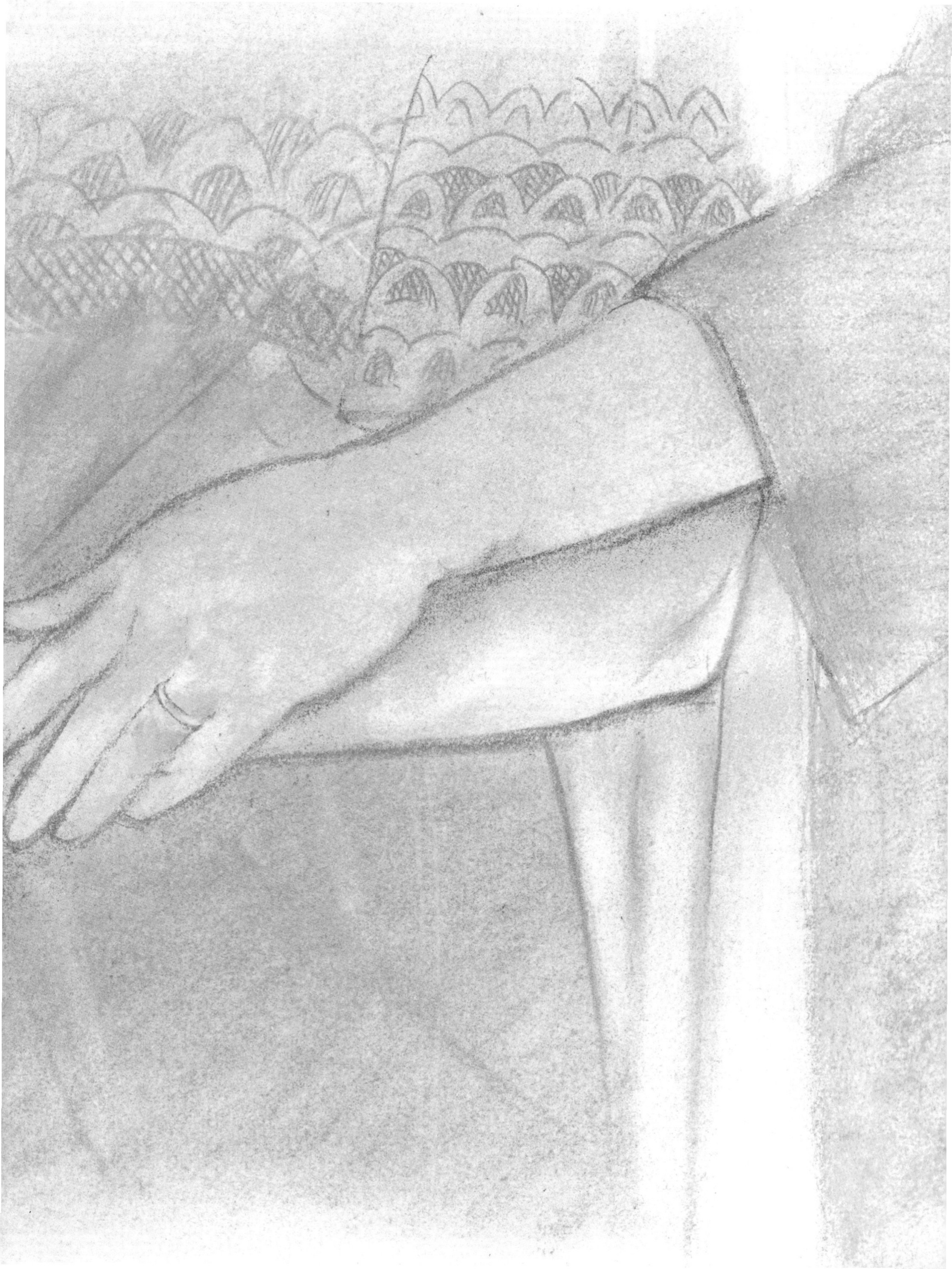

"Spring comes again.
Flowers bloom.
Leaves bud.
Robins make nests
and sing from the treetops
and leaves sing when the wind blows."

"In spring you were born."

"In spring I was born.
Mama, were you happy?"

"I hugged and kissed you.
And Daddy hugged and kissed you.
We were so happy.
And you know what?"

"What?"

"We still are."

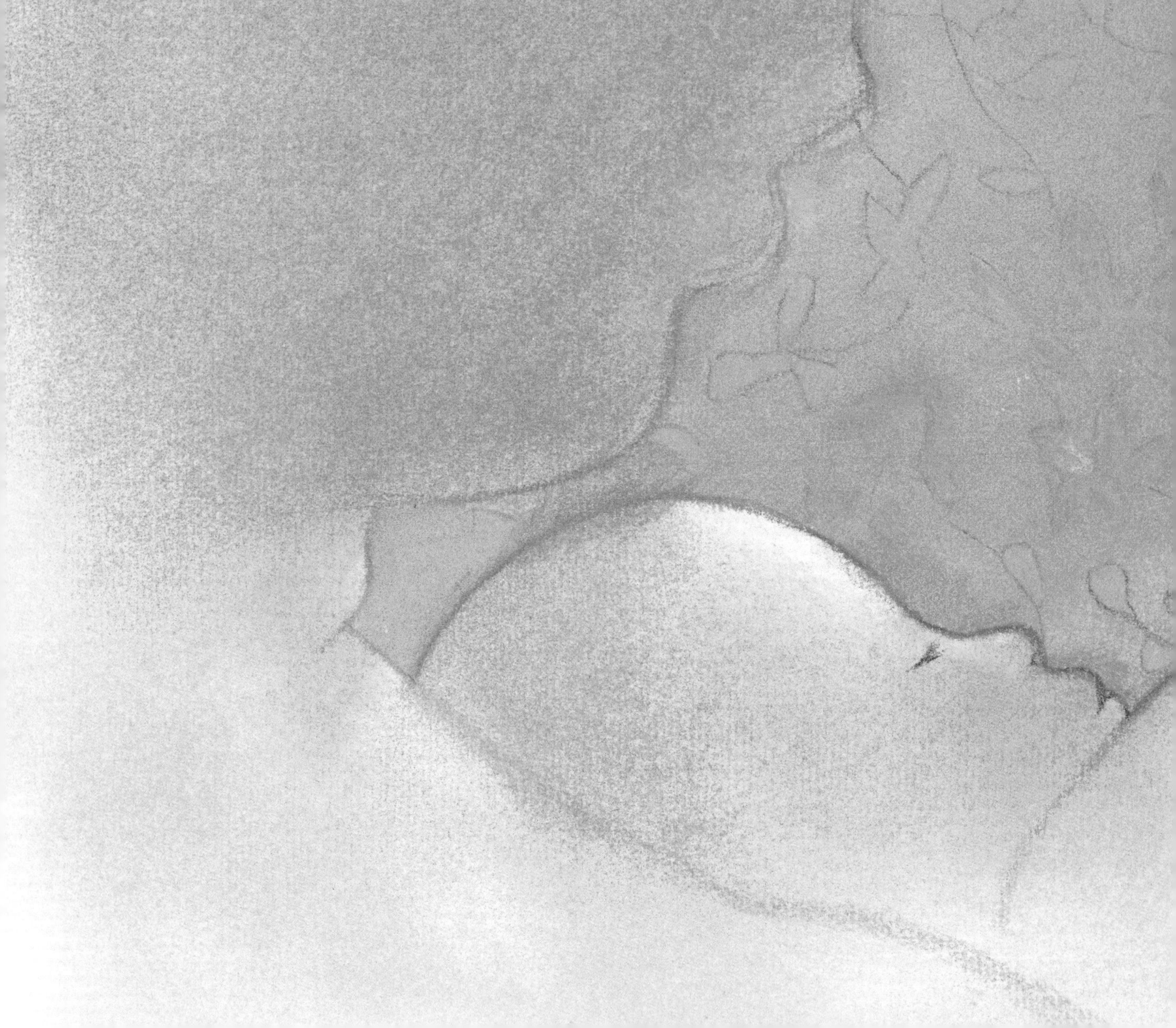

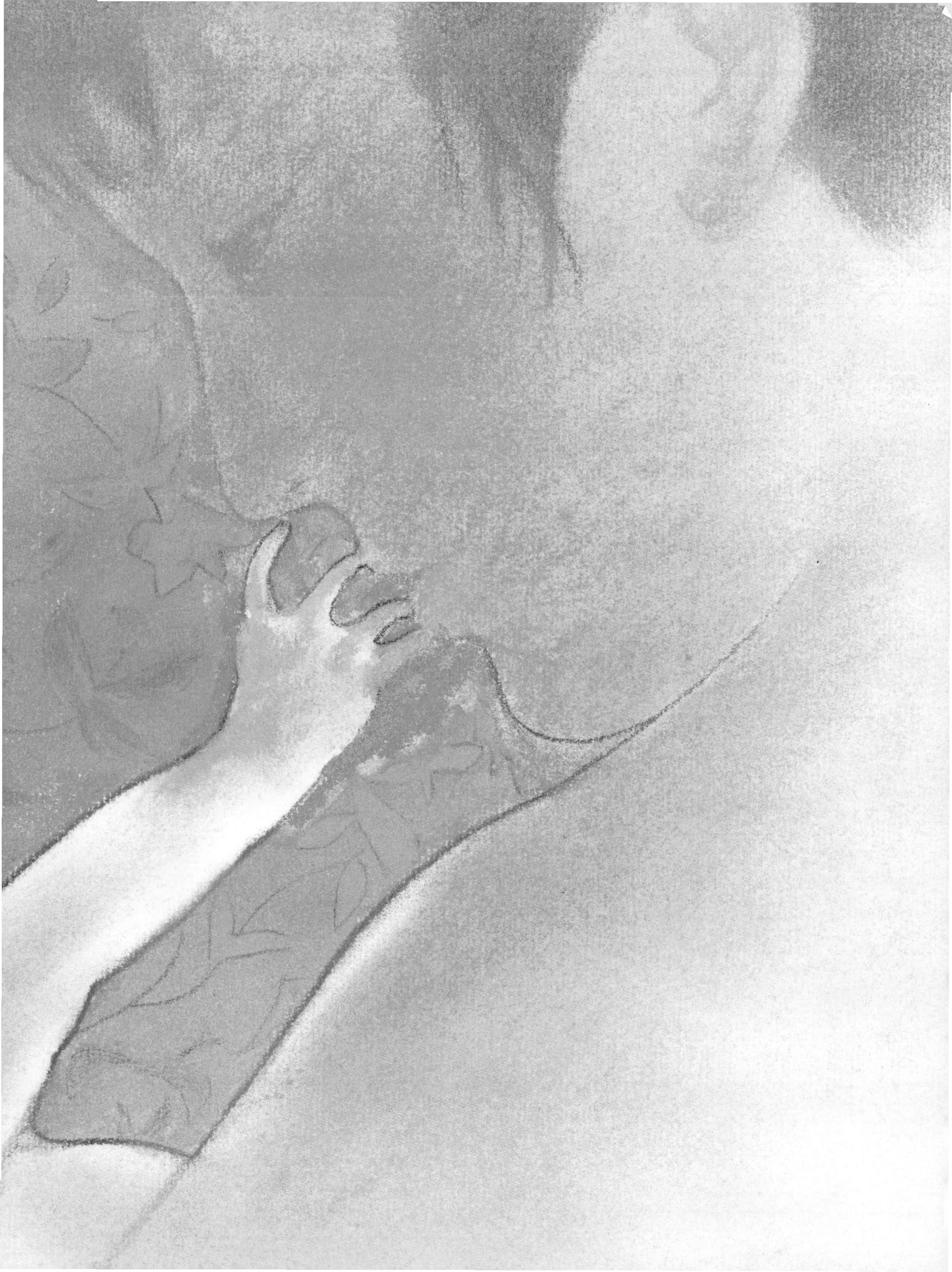